CLASSROOM CRITTERS

FRIENDS ALL DAY

by Molly Beth Griffin
illustrated by Colin Jack

CONTENTS

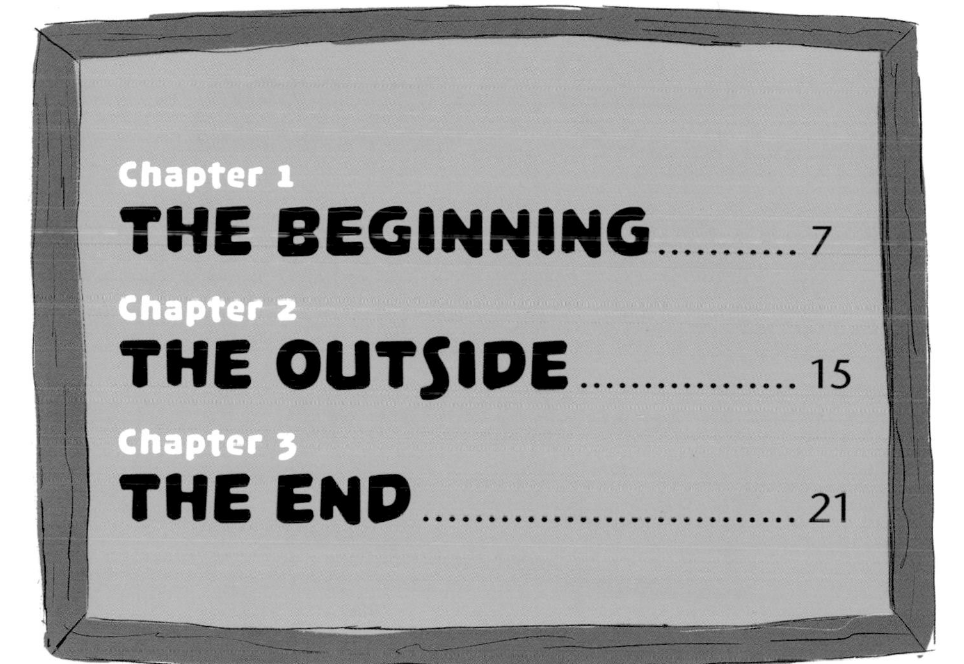

CLASSROOM CRITTERS

These five friends live within the walls, nooks and crannies of a primary school. They learn alongside the children every day, even though the children don't see them!

Stella is a mouse. She loves her friends. She also loves children and school! She came into the school on a cold winter's day. She knew it would be her home forever. Her favourite subjects are history and music. She is always eager for a new day to start.

Bo is a parakeet. He is a classroom pet. The friends let him out of his cage so they can play together. Bo loves to read. He goes home with his teacher at the weekend, but he always comes back to school to see his friends.

Delilah is a spider. She has always lived in the corners of the school. She is so small the children never notice her, but she is very clever. Delilah loves maths and computers and hates the broom!

Nico is a toad. He used to be a classroom pet. A child forgot to put him back into his tank one day. Now he lives with his friends. The whole school is his home! He can be grumpy, but he loves science and art. As Nico doesn't have fingers, he paints with his toes!

Goldie is a goldfish. She is very wise. The friends ask her questions when they have a big decision to make. She gives good advice and lives in the library.

Chapter 1

THE BEGINNING

Brinnnnnng! Stella the Mouse woke up with a jump. The first bell! She'd almost missed the best part of the day!

She scampered down the corridor to the front doors. She pressed her little nose against the cold glass. YES! There they were. The big school buses with children spilling out.

Stella loved children. She did not like how quiet the school was without them. She also did not like how still and dark the school was at night. Now the corridors were busy and loud.

Stella ran to get her best friends. She met up with Nico the Toad and Delilah the Spider first. Then the three friends picked up Bo the Parakeet.

They watched and waited as the children rushed past. Then they scampered and hopped and crept out from their hiding place.

Some of the children had breakfast before lessons. Stella and her friends were hungry too! They headed to the canteen.

They darted round the children's feet, grabbing spilt food. With full tummies, they went to lessons.

The friends liked different subjects. Stella liked history. Nico liked science. Delilah liked maths. Bo liked reading.

They kept well hidden. The friends did not let the children see them. They peeked out from behind rubbish bins.

They peered around cupboard doors. They listened from under curtains and on top of shelves. The friends loved learning.

Chapter 2

THE OUTSIDE

Lunch and playtime came quickly. The friends did not go outside. Outside it was cold and snowy.

"If we go out there, we might never get back in," Stella said.

Stella used to live outside. She knew what it was like to be cold, hungry and lonely. Nico, Delilah and Bo did not.

Nico used to be a classroom pet. Delilah had hatched in a corner of the staffroom. Bo was from a pet shop. He went home with his teacher at the weekend.

Now they were together, warm and safe. The school was their home. They were a family. Stella did not want to be cold, hungry or lonely ever again.

The friends all looked outside.

"The games look fun," said Stella. She had studied how groups of people work.

"But a storm is coming," said Nico. He had studied weather.

"And the clock says they'll come in soon. Playtime is almost over," said Delilah. She had studied time.

Bo looked at the sky. His wings twitched. He wanted to fly.

"Maybe I should go outside and try it," said Bo.

"I don't think that's a good idea," said Stella. "But let's go and ask Goldie for some advice."

Whenever the friends didn't know what to do, they went to see Goldie the Goldfish. She lived in the library. Goldie was very wise.

"Goldie, should Bo go outside?" asked Stella.

Goldie swam in a circle.

"Blub, blub," she said.

One blub meant "yes". Two blubs meant "no". At least, that's what the friends thought she meant.

"She's right," said Stella. "Outside you would be cold, hungry and lonely."

"True," Bo said. "Plus I love to read. There are no books outside."

Chapter 3
THE END

The children ran inside from playtime. Their cheeks were red. Their voices were happy. They went back to their lessons.

The animals were ready and waiting. They loved the afternoon at school. There were so many fun subjects.

Stella loved music lessons because she could sing. She liked to run across the piano keys at night, too.

Nico loved art lessons. He painted with his toes. Blue was his colour of choice in the winter.

Delilah loved the IT room. She was learning how to code.

Bo loved the library. He read stories. He read poems. He read the whole dinosaur section TWICE!

P.E. lessons were not safe for small animals. Balls flew and feet pounded.

The friends watched and tried to stay safe. It wasn't always easy!

At the end of the day, the children packed their backpacks and left. They stomped out of the front doors and climbed onto their school buses.

The kids were always happy to have finished the school day. Stella didn't understand why they liked to leave. She thought it was so much fun!

Stella watched from the window and sniffled a bit. The school was so quiet with no children.

"Let's go, Stella," said Nico.

"The broom will be here soon," said Delilah.

"And when the broom has gone," said Bo, "we can play the piano."

Stella smiled. Even without the children, she wasn't lonely. She had her friends. She had a home.

And besides, tomorrow the children would be back. Tomorrow the school would be busy and loud again.

Brinnnnnng! went the final bell.

15
30

TALK ABOUT IT

1. Each character has a different personality. Which one of the Classroom Critters would you be? Why?

2. This story takes place in the winter. Which words and illustrations show that?

3. Talk about your favourite subject at school (apart from lunch and playtime).

1. Go through the story and write down the schedule the children followed through the day. Compare it to your school day.

2. The five animals in this story are best friends. Write a paragraph about your best friends.

3. Pretend you're Goldie, and write a diary entry about your day.

Molly Beth Griffin is a writing teacher at the Loft Literary Center in Minneapolis, Minnesota, USA. She has written numerous picture books (including *Loon Baby* and *Rhoda's Rock Hunt)* and a YA novel *(Silhouette of a Sparrow)*. Molly loves reading and hiking in all kinds of weather. She lives in South Minneapolis with her partner and two children.

COLIN JACK

Colin Jack has illustrated several books for children, including *Little Miss Muffet* (Flip-Side Rhymes), *Jack and Jill* (Flip-Side Rhymes), *Dragons from Mars*, *7 Days of Awesome* and *If You Happen to Have a Dinosaur*. He also works as a story artist and character designer at DreamWorks Studios. Colin splits his time living in California, USA, and Canada with his wife and two children.

PLENTY OF CRITTERY FUN!
Discover more at
www.raintree.co.uk

A NEW YEAR
CLASSROOM CRITTERS
Welcome!
Feed Me
by Molly Beth Griffin
illustrated by Colin Jack
FRIENDS ALL DAY
CLASSROOM CRITTERS
by Molly Beth Griffin
illustrated by Colin Jack
PARTY TIME
CLASSROOM CRITTERS
by Molly Beth Griffin
illustrated by Colin Jack
PLANS GONE WRONG
CLASSROOM CRITTERS
by Molly Beth Griffin
illustrated by Colin Jack

Raintree is an imprint of Capstone Global Library Limited, a company incorporated in England and Wales having its registered office at 264 Banbury Road, Oxford, OX2 7DY – Registered company number: 6695582

www.raintree.co.uk
myorders@raintree.co.uk

Illustrated by Colin Jack
Designed by Ted Williams

Shutterstock: AVA Bitter, design element throughout,
Oleksandr Rybitskiy, design element throughout

Originated by Capstone Global Library Ltd
Printed and bound in India

ISBN 978 1 4747 7177 1

British Library Cataloguing in Publication Data:
A full catalogue record for this book is available from the British Library.